This book belongs to

Heather Watson

The
Puffin Book of
Five-minute
Animal Stories

The Puffin Book of Five-minute Animal Stories

Illustrated by Steve Cox

PUFFIN BOOKS

PUFFIN BOOKS

Published by the Penguin Group
Penguin Books Ltd, 27 Wrights Lane, London W8 5TZ, England
Penguin Putnam Inc., 375 Hudson Street, New York, New York 10014, USA
Penguin Books Australia Ltd, Ringwood, Victoria, Australia
Penguin Books Canada Ltd, 10 Alcorn Avenue, Toronto, Ontario, Canada M4V 3B2
Penguin Books India (P) Ltd, 11 Community Centre, Panchsheel Park, New Delhi – 110 017, India
Penguin Books (NZ) Ltd, Cnr Rosedale and Airborne Roads, Albany, Auckland, New Zealand
Penguin Books (South Africa) (Pty) Ltd, 5 Watkins Street, Denver Ext 4, Johannesburg 2094, South Africa

Penguin Books Ltd, Registered Offices: Harmondsworth, Middlesex, England

On the World Wide Web at: www.penguin.com

First published by Viking 1999
Published in Puffin Books 2001
1 3 5 7 9 10 8 6 4 2

The acknowledgements on page 124 constitute an extension of this copyright page

The moral right of the authors and illustrators has been asserted

Printed in Singapore by Imago Publishing Limited

British Library Cataloguing in Publication Data
A CIP catalogue record for this book is available from the British Library

ISBN 0–141–30416–2

CONTENTS

NORTY BOY

Dick King-Smith

HYLDA WAS AN old-fashioned sort of animal. She did not hold with the free and easy ways of the modern hedge-hog, and even preferred to call herself by the old name of 'hedgepig'. She planned to bring up her seven hedgepiglets very strictly.

'Children should be seen and not heard' was one of her favourite sayings, and 'Speak when you're spoken to' was another. She taught them to say 'Please' and 'Thank you', to eat nicely, to sniff quietly if their noses were running, and never to scratch in public, no matter how many fleas they had.

Six of them – three boys and three girls – grew up to be well behaved, with beautiful manners, but the seventh was a great worry to Hylda and her husband, Herbert. This seventh hedgepiglet was indeed the despair of Hylda's life. He was not only seen but constantly heard, speaking whether he was spoken to or not, and he never said 'Please' or 'Thank you'. He gobbled his food in a revolting, slobbery way, he sniffed very loudly indeed, and he was forever scratching.

His real name was Norton, but he was more often known as Norty.

Now some mother animals can wallop their young ones if they do not do what they are told. A lioness can cuff her cub, a monkey can clip its child round the ear, or an elephant can give her baby a biff with her trunk. But it's not so easy for hedgehogs.

'Sometimes,' said Hylda to Herbert, 'I wish that hedgepigs didn't have prickles.'

'Why is that, my dear?' said Herbert.

'Because then I could give our Norty a good hiding. He deserves it.'

'Why is that, my dear?' said Herbert.

'Not only is he disobedient, he has taken to answering me back. Why can't he be good like the others? Never have I known such a hedgepiglet. I shall be glad when November comes.'

'Why is that, my dear?' said Herbert.

Hylda sighed. Conversation with my husband, she said to herself for the umpteenth time, can hardly be called interesting.

'Because then it's time to hibernate, of course, and we can all have a good sleep. For five blissful months I shall not have to listen to that impudent, squeaky, little voice arguing, complaining, refusing to do what I say and generally giving me cheek.'

Hylda should have known it would not be that easy.

When November came, she said to her husband and the seven children, 'Come along, all of you.'

'Yes, Mummy,' said the three good boys and the three good girls, and, 'Why is that, my dear?' said Herbert, but Norty only said, 'Shan't.'

'Norty,' said Hylda, 'if you do not do what you are told, I

shall get your father to give you a good hard smack.'

Norty fluffed up his spines and sniggered.

'You'll be sorry if you do, Dad,' he said.

'Where are we going, Mummy?' asked one of the hedgepiglets.

'We are going to find a nice deep bed of dry leaves where we can hibernate.'

'What does "hibernate" mean, Mummy?' asked another.

'It means to go to sleep, all through the winter. When it's rainy and blowy and frosty and snowy outside, we shall all be fast asleep under the leaf pile, all cosy and warm. Won't that be lovely?'

'No,' said Norty.

'Norton!' said his mother angrily. 'Are you coming or are you not?'

'No,' said Norty.

'Oh well, stay here then,' snapped Hylda, 'and freeze to death!' And she trotted off with the rest.

In a far corner of the garden they found a nice deep bed of dry leaves, and Hylda and Herbert and the six good hedgepiglets burrowed their way into it, curled up tight, shut their eyes and went to sleep.

The following April they woke up, opened their eyes, uncurled and burrowed out into the spring sunshine.

'Goodbye, Mummy. Goodbye, Daddy,' chorused the six good hedgepiglets, and off they trotted to seek their fortunes.

'Oh, Herbert,' said Hylda. 'I feel so sad.'

'Why is that, my dear?' said Herbert.

'I should never have left our Norty out in the cold last November. He will have frozen to death, poor little fellow. What does it matter that he was rude and disobedient and cheeky? Oh, if only I could hear his squeaky voice again, I'd be the happiest hedgepig ever!'

At that moment there was a rustling from the other side of the bed of leaves, and out came Norty.

'Can't you keep your voices down?' he said, yawning. 'A fellow can't get a wink of sleep.'

'Norty!' cried Hylda. 'You did hibernate after all!'

''Course I did,' said Norty. 'What did you expect me to do – freeze to death?'

'Oh, my Norty boy!' said Hylda. 'Are you all right?'

'I was,' said Norty, 'till you woke me, nattering on as usual.'

'Now, now,' said Hylda, controlling herself with difficulty, 'that's not the way to speak to your mother, is it? Come here

and give me a kiss.'

'Don't want to,' said Norty.

'Anyone would think,' said Hylda, 'that you weren't pleased to see us.'

'Anyone,' said Norty, 'would be right.'

'Well, push off then!' shouted Hylda. 'Your brothers and sisters have all gone, so get lost!'

'Shan't,' said Norty.

He yawned again, full in his mother's face.

'I'm going back to bed,' he said. 'So there.'

At this Hylda completely lost her temper.

'I've had enough!' she screamed. 'You're the rudest hedgepig in the world and your father's the most boring, and I never want to see either of you again!' And she ran away as fast as she could go.

Herbert and Norty stared after her. Norty scratched his fleas and sniffed very noisily.

'Looks like she's done a bunk, Dad,' he said.

'Yes,' said Herbert. 'Why is that, my dear?'

'Can't think,' said Norty. 'But then she always was prickly.'

FETCH THE SLIPPER

Sheila Lavelle

GRANDAD CAME DOWNSTAIRS one morning looking very cross and grumpy.

He looked as grumpy as a giraffe with a sore throat.

'I've lost one of my slippers,' he grumbled. 'One of my best red velvet slippers that Betty sent from America. Now what am I going to do?'

'Put your wellies on instead,' said Mum.

Grandad scowled.

'Ha-ha! Very funny,' he said. 'You're some help, I must say!'

He sat down at the kitchen table.

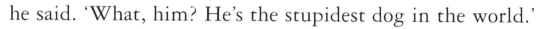

Jamie and Fiona giggled into their cornflakes.

Dad poured some tea into Grandad's cup.

'Don't worry, Grandad,' he said. 'Benbow will find it.'

Grandad scowled. 'Benbow?' he said. 'What, him? He's the stupidest dog in the world.'

'He's very good at finding things,' said Mum.

She gave Grandad a plate of bacon and eggs.

Jamie and Fiona began to shout, 'Benbow! Benbow! Where are you?'

A big collie dog with muddy paws came running in from the garden.

He was black and white and brown, with a bushy tail that never stopped wagging.

Benbow liked fetching things better than anything else in the world.

'Fetch the slipper, Benbow,' said Grandad.

Benbow wagged his tail.

He ran happily out of the kitchen and bounded up the stairs.

Benbow was back in no time with a red velvet slipper in his mouth.

'I told you so,' said Mum smugly.

Grandad looked at the slipper.

'That's the left slipper, you mutt!' he said. 'It's the right one that's missing!'

Fiona giggled so much she almost choked.

Grandad flung the slipper on the floor.

Jamie buttered a slice of toast.

'Try again, Benbow,' he said. 'Fetch the *other* slipper.'

Benbow raced out again.

He was back in no time with Jamie's old green shirt that had no buttons on.

'I haven't seen that for years!' laughed Jamie. 'Fetch the SLIPPER, Benbow.'

With a joyful bark Benbow dashed upstairs.

This time he came back with a pink plastic lavatory brush.

'I've been looking for that for weeks!' said Mum in amazement.

Everybody laughed and Benbow galloped out again.

He came back a minute later with Dad's red woolly nightcap.

'Now where on earth did he find that?' said Dad, scratching his head.

'FETCH THE SLIPPER, BENBOW!' everybody shouted together, and Benbow raced out once more.

This was the best game he had ever played in his life.

Soon Benbow had made a huge pile of things on the kitchen floor.

He was puffing and panting and his tongue was hanging out of his mouth.

But he still hadn't found Grandad's slipper.

Jamie put his arms round Benbow's neck.

He looked straight into the dog's eyes.

'Slipper, Benbow!' he said. 'Slipper! Fetch the SLIPPER!'

Benbow looked at Jamie, his head on one side.

Suddenly Benbow turned and raced out of the kitchen door.

He galloped down the garden path.

He leaped over the gate and bounded down the lane towards the village.

NOW he knew what everybody wanted.

'What on earth can he be up to?' said Mum, pouring another cup of tea.

'Something stupid, I'll bet,' grumbled Grandad.

Jamie and Fiona went out into the garden to wait for Benbow to come back.

They didn't have to wait long. Benbow came flying over the garden gate and raced towards the house.

Something was dangling from his jaws. Something brown and slippery.

'What can it be?' said Fiona.

Benbow sat down proudly at Jamie's feet.

Jamie took the slippery brown thing out of the dog's mouth.

He laughed so much he almost fell over.

'That's not a slipper, Benbow,' he said. 'It's a KIPPER!'

'Yuck!' said Fiona, making a face.

Mum gave the kipper to the cat.

'I told you Benbow was a stupid dog,' snorted Grandad.

He sat in his old armchair and sulked.

Benbow looked sad and hung his head. Jamie felt sorry for him.

'Never mind, Benbow,' he said. 'You did your best. Let's go and play in the garden.'

Jamie threw Benbow's rubber ball down the lawn and Benbow brought it back.

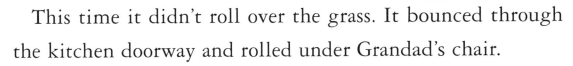

'Good dog!' said Jamie.

Benbow wagged his tail.

'My turn now,' said Fiona.

She threw the ball.

This time it didn't roll over the grass. It bounced through the kitchen doorway and rolled under Grandad's chair.

'What a rotten throw!' said Jamie.

'Fetch the ball, Benbow,' said Fiona.

Benbow ran into the kitchen.

He lay on the floor and put his head under Grandad's chair.

He wriggled out with something in his mouth.

It wasn't the ball.

It was Grandad's lost slipper.

The red velvet one that Betty had sent from America.

It had been under Grandad's chair all the time.

'Grandad!' laughed Jamie. 'Benbow has found your slipper!'

Everybody hugged and patted Benbow.

Even Grandad began to smile.

'He's the cleverest dog in the world,' he said. 'Haven't I always said so?'

THE POCKET ELEPHANT

Catherine Sefton

MARY HAD AN ELEPHANT that lived in her cardigan pocket. The pocket was special. It was an elephant pocket.

The pocket was lined with lettuce leaves for the elephant to eat, and sometimes Mary fed it bread and jam, which made the pocket and the elephant sticky.

One day Mary took her elephant to school.

'Good morning, Mary,' said Miss Wiley, her teacher.

'Good morning, Miss Wiley,' said Mary. 'I've brought my elephant to school.'

'Why have you brought your elephant to school, Mary?'

asked Miss Wiley.

'There are lots of books about elephants in school,' said Mary. 'I thought my elephant might like to read one.'

'Right!' said Miss Wiley, and she got out an elephant book. Mary put the book in her elephant pocket for the elephant to read.

The elephant settled down to read it. The more it read, the more amazed the elephant was.

The book wasn't about elephants in special pockets, it was about elephants in jungles, with lions and tigers to play with, and banana leaves to eat, as well as bananas!

Mary went to eat her school lunch, and she left her cardigan hanging on the back of her chair.

When she came back she got out the bread and jam from her lunchbox to feed the elephant BUT . . . the elephant had gone!

'Has anybody seen my elephant?' Mary asked anxiously. 'It's a small sticky one.'

Nobody had.

'ELEPHANT! ELEPHANT!' Mary shouted. Everybody else

started shouting too, and running about the school looking for elephants.

There was a trail of small jammy elephant footprints running down the hall and over the mat and out the door.

'My elephant went that way!' Mary cried, and everyone ran after it.

The elephant footprints stopped at the edge of the grass. By the time the elephant got there, the jam had all rubbed off.

Where was the elephant?

It was deep in the grass, like a big elephant in the jungle.

It didn't find any lions or tigers or bananas, but it found some ants and a centipede and a ladybird, and played with them. The elephant ate a bit of daisy, which it liked, and tried a bit of nettle which it didn't like, because the nettle stung its trunk.

Meanwhile all the children and Miss Wiley and Mary were elephant-hunting, but there was a lot of grass and not a lot of elephant to look for, and they didn't find it.

They had to give up, and go back to school. Mary cried, because she had lost her elephant.

The elephant didn't know that. It was having a great time playing with a mouse.

They played and they played and they played.

'I really must go home now,' said the mouse.

The elephant went with it, but when they got to the mouse's house, the elephant couldn't get in. The mousehole was too small for the elephant.

And it was getting dark. *And* it was getting cold. *And* it was getting late. And . . . and . . . *AND* . . . there was a CAT!

It was like the tiger in the elephant's book, but *bigger*, and it hadn't read the book, and didn't know about elephants. It thought it was chasing a funny kind of mouse.

The elephant ran, and so did the cat and WOOOOOOOOOOOOOOOOFFF!!!!!

There was a dog!

It didn't know about elephants either, but it knew about cats. The dog chased the cat and the elephant and SCCRAMMMMMM!

There was a man.

He chased the cat and the dog, and saved the elephant, just in time.

'What a small elephant!' he said, and he popped it in his pocket.

The man's pocket wasn't *meant* as a pocket for elephants. It had nuts and screws and bolts and a handkerchief in it, but the elephant didn't mind. It was much happier being back in a pocket than it had been running about in the jungle outside, which is what it thought the grass *was*, because it had never been in a real jungle.

Then

'E-l-e-p-h-a-n-t! E-l-e-p-h-a-n-t!'

The elephant heard a voice that it knew, and it started to wriggle and bounce in the pocket.

It was Mary and Miss Wiley, having a last after-school look for the elephant!

'Pardon me, madam,' said the man. 'Have you lost an elephant?'

'Yes,' said Miss Wiley.

'It was small and sort of sticky,' Mary said.

'And frightened!' said the man, and he took the elephant

out of his pocket.

Mary saw the elephant, and the elephant saw Mary, both at the same time.

The elephant hopped off the man's hand and ran down Mary's arms and popped into its own special pocket. The elephant lay there, with its small elephant heart pounding and pounding!

Mary took the elephant home, and they both went to bed.

The elephant didn't *stay* in its pocket this time, as it did most nights. Mary took it into bed with her, because it was small, and still very frightened.

They both read the elephant's book, and Mary explained about jungles being great places for big elephants, but not-so-good for *small* elephants that live in pockets.

'But I'll be big some day, won't I?' the elephant said.

'Yes, you will,' said Mary.

'Then I can live in the jungle!' said the elephant.

And they both went to sleep thinking about it.

RUBY, THE CAR-BOOT RHINO

Rhiannon Powell

ONE WEEKEND, RALPH and his parents went to a car boot sale. There were a lot of cars and vans. Men and women were selling all sorts of things from open boots and on tables. They were things that people didn't need any more – but hoped that other people might want to buy.

Ralph was excited! He saw all kinds of interesting objects, and most were not expensive. His mum and dad had given him one pound to spend. He wandered among the cars wondering what to buy.

Ralph saw bicycles with no wheels, and wheels with no

bicycles! He saw old clothes — from furry boots to swimming costumes. He saw bath taps, tools, toys, books, bags, balls, paintings, pushchairs, pots and pans — even a kitchen sink!

Ralph came to a big van that was bursting with strange and interesting things. There was a brightly painted tall clock, some funny hats on a hat-stand, some very unusual plants, odd shoes, stuffed animals, a treasure chest, masks, musical instruments — and lots more.

In between the tall clock and the hat-stand Ralph noticed a strange, grey, pointed object. What was it?

He looked more closely . . . Suddenly — on the other side of the hat-stand — an eye opened! It looked straight at Ralph — and winked!

Then Ralph realized what he was staring at.

It was a RHINOCEROS!!

It winked again and smiled. Ralph smiled back.

A little man appeared from behind the treasure chest.

'How much is the rhinoceros, please?' Ralph asked politely.

The man looked thoughtful for a moment.

'Mmm – Ruby the rhino – Let me see . . .' He turned to Ralph. 'She's yours for a pound,' he said, smiling.

It was Ralph's lucky day! His mum had told him not to spend all his money at once – but this was a bargain!

Ralph led Ruby out of the van and went to look for his mum and dad.

'Look what I've bought!' he said excitedly, finding them at a cake stall. 'She's called Ruby!'

They could not believe their eyes!

'I know you like unusual things, Ralph,' said Dad, 'but this is . . .'

'. . . is very BIG!' finished Mum.

After a lot of pleading from Ralph, his parents were finally persuaded to keep Ruby – if they could get her home!

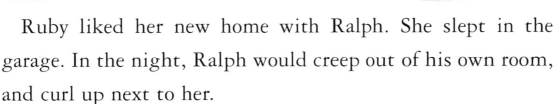

Their car was not very big, but it had a roof that opened, so, with plenty of pushing and pulling, Ruby was squeezed in – and home they all went!

Ruby liked her new home with Ralph. She slept in the garage. In the night, Ralph would creep out of his own room, and curl up next to her.

Ralph lived by a big park. It soon became Ruby's favourite place. There was lots of open space, plenty of twigs and leaves to eat, water and mud to roll around in, and crowds of children to play with.

Ruby was not very good on the swings and slides. She was too heavy and clumsy, but she always tried, and she and Ralph would have a good giggle!

Only Ruby could get Ralph up really high on the see-saw, and she was very good at towing in the rowing boats that got stuck in the middle of the park lake!

Ruby liked to play tennis with Ralph. She often missed the ball (rhinos have poor eyesight), but when she hit it, she was so strong, the racket would break and the ball would vanish out of sight!

Ruby tried roller-skating with Ralph and his friends. She needed two pairs of roller-skates, and a push to start her off. The only way she could stop was by falling over – knocking the others down like skittles! Everyone had great fun!

The people in the park loved Ruby. She took dogs for walks, gave children rides, and played in the lake with the ducks. She and Ralph made lots of new friends.

One sunny afternoon, Ralph and Ruby and some friends were chatting with Stan the park-keeper. Suddenly, Ruby's ears pricked up . . . in the distance she could hear a little voice screaming, 'HELP!'

Ruby galloped off towards the sound of the cries! She saw that a small girl had fallen into the stream that ran out of the lake. The water was deep and flowing fast, and the girl could not swim!

Ruby thundered on to the bridge that crossed the stream, and bravely stretched right out over the side!

Ralph and the others, breathless from chasing her, gripped on to her tail and back legs.

'Careful, Ruby!' cried Ralph.

Ruby scooped her horn into the water just in time to gently hook the little girl to safety and into her mother's arms!

The crowd that had gathered around clapped and cheered!

Ruby blushed – ruby red!

The next day, the newspaper printed a big photograph of Ralph and Ruby.

RUBY TO THE RESCUE! read the front page!

Ralph was very proud. His unusual boot sale bargain was the bravest, biggest, best friend a boy could have!

THE THREE LITTLE PIGS

Traditional

ONCE UPON A TIME there was an old sow with three little pigs, and she sent them out to seek their fortune.

The first little pig met a man who gave him a bundle of straw and he built a house with it.

Then along came a wolf who knocked at the door and said, 'Little pig, little pig, let me come in.'

And the little pig answered, 'No, no, by the hair on my chinny chin chin!'

'Then I'll huff and I'll puff and I'll blow your house in!' said the wolf.

So the wolf huffed and he puffed and he blew the house in and he ate up the little pig.

The second little pig met a man who gave him a bundle of sticks and he built his house with them.

Then along came the wolf who knocked at the door and said, 'Little pig, little pig, let me come in.'

And the little pig answered, 'No, no, by the hair on my chinny chin chin!'

'Then I'll huff and I'll puff and I'll blow your house in!' said the wolf.

The wolf huffed and he puffed and he huffed and he puffed and he blew the house in and he ate up the little pig.

The third little pig met a man who gave him a pile of bricks and he built his house with them.

Then the wolf came, just as he had to the other little pigs, and he knocked on the door and said, 'Little pig, little pig, let me come in.'

And the little pig answered, 'No, no, by the hair on my chinny chin chin!'

So the wolf said, 'Then I'll huff and I'll puff and I'll blow your house in!'

Well, the wolf huffed and he puffed and he puffed and he huffed and he huffed and he puffed but he could *not* blow that house down. So he said to the little pig, 'Little pig, I know where there are some nice turnips.'

'Where?' said the little pig.

'Down in Farmer Smith's field,' said the wolf. 'If you will be ready tomorrow morning at six o'clock I will come and get you, and we can pick some turnips together.'

'Very well,' said the little pig, and the wolf went away.

The next morning the little pig got up at five o'clock and picked some turnips before the wolf came round at six.

When the wolf arrived he said, 'Are you ready, little pig?'

'I have been there and back and have enough turnips for dinner,' said the little pig.

The wolf was very angry at this but he said in his nicest voice, 'Little pig, I know where there is a fine apple tree.'

'Where?' said the little pig.

'Over in Mary's garden,' said the wolf. 'And if you will not trick me, I will come for you tomorrow morning at five o'clock and we will pick some apples.'

Well, the little pig got up at four o'clock the next morning, hoping to pick the apples and get back home before the wolf arrived. But he had further to go this time and he saw the wolf just as he was climbing down from the apple tree.

The wolf stood under the tree and said, 'Why, little pig, you are here before me! Are they nice apples?'

'Oh, yes,' said the little pig, 'they are good and sweet. Here, I will throw one down to you.'

And he threw the apple so far that while the wolf went to get it, the little pig jumped down from the tree and ran home.

The next day, the wolf came again and said to the little pig, 'Little pig, will you go to the fair with me this afternoon?'

'Oh yes,' said the little pig. 'What time will you come to get me?'

'I will come at three,' said the wolf.

So the little pig left early, as usual, and bought a butter churn at the fair. He was walking home with it when he saw the wolf coming. The little pig was scared and he hopped inside the butter churn to hide. But the butter

churn

tipped over

and rolled down the hill

with the little pig inside. And it

rolled right down towards the wolf and the wolf

was so frightened that he ran away and never went to the fair.

Later, the wolf went back to the little pig's house and told him about the big scary thing chasing him down the hill.

'Ha! So I scared you,' the little pig laughed from inside his house. 'That was the butter churn I bought at the fair and I was inside it.'

When he heard this, the wolf was very, *very* angry and he said that he was coming down the chimney to eat up the little pig.

The little pig quickly filled a large pot with water and put it on the blazing fire. The wolf came down the chimney and fell straight into the boiling water. The little pig put the lid on the pot, boiled up the wolf and ate him for his supper and he lived happily ever after.

PLAIN JACK

K. M. Peyton

ONCE THERE WERE two old mares in a field together, who each had a foal.

One mare had won a lot of races and thought a lot of herself. She spoilt her foal dreadfully.

She told him how clever he was and what a lot of races he would win when he grew up.

He was very valuable and called Fire of England.

The other mare was very plain and

had won only one small race. Her foal was plain, like her, and called Plain Jack.

'You will have to work very hard if you are to be a winner, Plain Jack,' she said to him sternly. 'You don't come from a family of great winners like Fire. All the same,' she added tartly, 'he'll come to a bad end if he doesn't behave himself.'

Jack remembered her words, and when they went to the sales he behaved his very best. But he only fetched a small price. He was bought by a man called Bill who lived in the North.

But Fire, in spite of behaving disgracefully in the sale-ring, was sold for an enormous price to a very rich owner, and went to live in the best stable in England.

'I will try very hard to make Bill pleased with me,' thought Jack.

A lad called Barney looked after him and his jockey was called Joe. They liked Plain Jack because he tried. When he was ready to race they took him to Yarmouth. To Jack's surprise he found Fire was entered in the same race.

Fire was ridden by the best jockey in the country. Everyone admired him. But he was very naughty and bucked his jockey off. The crowd booed and someone threw a tomato.

But Plain Jack tried his hardest and came fifth out of twenty-three horses.

Bill and Joe and Barney were very pleased with him.

Every time he ran, Plain Jack tried his hardest, and the crowd liked him because he never let them down.

Barney read to Jack from the racing paper: 'Plain Jack is a great favourite with the racing public.'

But on the back page it said: 'Fire of England disappointment.' It said Fire was to be sold because he was no good.

Plain Jack did not see him again

until he was sent to run in a race at Epsom.

The racecourse was on the downs, and people were picnicking and playing cricket. Some children were riding along by the rails.

One of the horses was a very thin, poor chestnut. When it saw Plain Jack going down to the start of the race, it put up its head and whinnied. Jack got a great surprise, recognizing his old friend Fire.

Jack did not want to race, he wanted to stay with Fire. When the race started Jack hung back. Joe did not know what was wrong with him. Fire bucked his rider off just like old times, jumped the rails and chased after the race. He ran like the wind.

'Look at that thin old nag!' everyone laughed. 'He's the fastest of the lot!'

But at the end Fire was caught and led away in disgrace.

Plain Jack had come last and Bill and Joe and Barney were

very disappointed with him. It was the first bad race he had ever run.

They took him home but Plain Jack would not eat and stood with his head in the corner thinking of poor Fire.

He got very thin. Bill called the vet but the vet could find nothing wrong with him.

'I don't understand it,' said Bill. 'Ever since Epsom –'

Barney had an idea. He told Joe to go to Epsom to try to find out about the thin chestnut horse who seemed to have upset Jack so. Joe searched all the riding stables and found Fire at last in a grotty shed with no food and no water. He was thinner than before and very miserable.

Joe examined him carefully.

'Why! You're Fire of England – I recognize you! The day the guv'nor bought Jack, you were sold for half a million pounds! But you're not worth tuppence now.'

Joe told Bill and Bill bought Fire from his nasty owner. Joe fetched Fire home. When he walked in the yard, Plain Jack put his head out of his box and whinnied with excitement.

Bill laughed. 'So that was the trouble! Put him in the box next to Jack, and get them each a good feed! I can use Fire for my hack.'

Barney brought two big feeds. Both horses ate up every oat – and wanted more!

So Fire of England came back into a racing stable and grew fat and happy again. Plain Jack went on running races, trying his hardest and never giving in, and the racing public loved him because he never let them down, except that one time.

When Fire and Jack got old and were retired, they were turned out in a field together. They stood under the trees in the shade, swishing their tails – the horse with a great talent who never used it, and the horse with little talent who used it all.

Sophie and the Wonderful Picture

Kaye Umansky

Sophie Rabbit and Graham Frog had painted a wonderful picture.

It had taken them all morning, and they had used up nearly all the green paint, but Mrs Badger said it was worth it.

'Look, everyone!' cried Mrs Badger when she saw it. 'Just stop for a moment, and look at this lovely painting. What is it, you two?'

'It's the pond where I live,' explained Graham. 'That's my lily pad there, look. And those green blobs are all my relations. Sophie painted those. Go on, Sophie, tell them.'

Sophie blushed and shook her head.

'You do it, Graham,' she whispered. 'You're so much better at explaining things than me.'

So Graham explained all about the painting. He did it so well that when he finished, the class clapped.

'Tomorrow, your mums and dads will be coming to see the end of term assembly,' said Mrs Badger. 'Would you like to show your painting?'

'Yes please,' said Graham immediately.

But Sophie wasn't so sure.

'I'm scared of standing up in front of everyone,' she confided to Graham. 'I'll feel shy. All those eyes staring at me!'

'Don't worry,' said Graham. 'I'll do all the talking. All you have to do is hold it the right way up.'

'Are you coming to assembly tomorrow?' Sophie asked her mum and dad when she got home.

'Of course, love,' said her mum.

'Wild ferrets wouldn't keep me away,' said Sophie's dad. 'Especially now I know our Soph's the star.'

'I'm not doing much,' said Sophie 'Just holding up a painting. Graham's doing all the talking. My bit's not at all important.'

But that night, Sophie couldn't get to sleep.

'What's up, Soph?' asked her dad when he came to tuck her in. 'Is it stage fright?'

Sophie nodded.

'Suppose I hold it upside down?' she whispered. 'What if I drop it?'

'You won't,' said George Rabbit. 'But if you do, just keep smiling. You can get away with most things if you've got a big smile on your face.'

The following morning, the school hall was crammed with everyone's relations.

Sophie's mum and dad arrived early, and sat near the door so that Gareth could be taken out if he played up. Sophie's dad gave her a big wink, and Sophie gave him a timid little wave.

As for Graham's relations – well! They took up the whole front row looking proud enough to burst.

'Good morning, everyone,' said Mrs Badger. 'To start our

show, Gordon Fox, Andrew Otter and Rebecca Water-Rat will do a dance entitled *Falling Leaves*.'

Gordon, Andrew and Rebecca stood up, Mrs Badger took her place at the piano, and the show began.

The Falling Leaves danced beautifully, and got a big clap.

So did Kelly and Fran Mouse, when they sang their cheese song.

Terry Tortoise showed a fishing rod he had made, and everyone nodded and said how clever he was.

Then it was Graham and Sophie's turn.

'Graham and Sophie will now tell you all about their new picture,' said Mrs Badger.

Sophie's mum and dad craned their necks.

Graham's relations sat up straight, and nudged each other excitedly.

'Stand up, you two. Hold it up high, Sophie, so everyone can see,' said Mrs Badger.

Heart in her mouth, Sophie stood up and held the picture high.

'Come on, Graham,' she

whispered. 'Stand up! It's our turn.'

But Graham didn't move.

To everyone's surprise, he just sat there.

His face looked a paler green than usual.

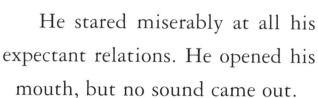

He stared miserably at all his expectant relations. He opened his mouth, but no sound came out.

Desperately, he rolled his eyes at Sophie, and shook his head.

'Can't!' he said, in a small, strangled voice.

It was true. Graham couldn't.

'All right,' whispered Sophie. 'You do the holding. I'll do the talking.'

Gratefully, Graham stood up, took the picture, and held it high.

Sophie caught George Rabbit's eye. She took a deep breath, gave a wobbly smile, and began to speak.

'This is a painting we did of Graham's pond,' she said, in a clear voice. 'This is Graham's lily pad, and this is a mayfly, and these are reeds. And these are all his relations . . . '

And Sophie told the audience all about the painting, while

Graham held it as high as he possibly could.

When she had finished, there came a storm of applause.

Graham's relations stood up and cheered, and so did Sophie's mum and dad. Even Gareth joined in.

'Thanks, Sophie. I'm sorry about that,' whispered Graham. 'It was all those eyes, staring at me!'

'I know what you mean,' said Sophie, waving at her mum and dad, who were still clapping their paws off.

'You were really good,' said Graham. 'I thought you said you were shy?'

'I was,' said Sophie, her eyes shining. 'Once. But not any more.'

THE PERSISTENT SNAIL

Linda Allen

ONCE THERE WAS a very old woman who grew lettuces in her garden. Every morning she watered them, and every afternoon she picked one for her tea.

One day she went out to water her lettuces and found that they had been nibbled around the edges. 'Snails!' she cried. 'There are snails in my garden nibbling my lettuces!' The old woman searched for snails all day, but she did not find any.

In fact there was only one snail in her garden, but he had a very big appetite. On his shell was a curious mark, like the wings of a butterfly. No other snail had a shell like his.

He only came out at night. In the day he stayed fast asleep in a hole in the wall.

That night the old woman went out with a lantern to look for him. She found him nibbling one of her lettuces. 'So it's you!' she said. 'I knew I would catch you by the light of my lantern.'

She was a kind old woman who never killed anything, so she put the snail in a box and carried him out into the lane. She walked along the lane for a mile until she came to a garden wall. 'There you are,' she said to the snail. 'I am sure you will

find something to eat around here. Goodbye and good luck to you!' Then she went home.

At first the snail was rather confused. But he could smell something delicious not very far away. He slid down the wall and went to look for it. In the garden behind the wall he found the most scrumptious cabbages he had ever tasted.

In the morning the old man who lived there came out to look at his cabbages. 'Snails!' he shouted. 'There are snails in my garden eating my cabbages.' But there was only one snail . . . who had found a hole in the wall and was fast asleep. The old man couldn't find him.

That night the old man went out with a lantern and searched. At

last he found the snail with the curious mark on his shell. 'It's you!' he cried. 'You'd better come with me.'

He put the snail in his pocket and walked a mile up the lane until he came to the old woman's garden wall. 'There you are,' he said, taking the snail out of his pocket. 'Eat what you find in there and don't you trouble me again.' Then he went home.

Next morning the old woman went to water her lettuces. 'Another snail!' she said. 'Well, I will find him tonight, and then I'll take him to where I took the other one I found.'

She was amazed to find that it was the very same snail. 'How did you get back here so quickly?' she said. 'I never knew that snails could travel so fast.' Once again she put him

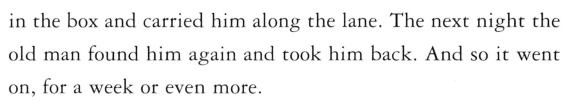

in the box and carried him along the lane. The next night the old man found him again and took him back. And so it went on, for a week or even more.

One day the old man and the old woman met in the lane. It was raining. 'I am glad it is raining,' said the old woman. 'I shall not have to water my lettuces today.'

'And I shall not have to water my cabbages,' said the old man. Then he told the old woman what had been happening to him.

'That's very odd!' exclaimed the old woman. 'The very same thing has been happening to me.'

'What does your snail look like?' asked the old man.

'Oh,' said the old woman, 'he has a mark on his shell like the wings of a butterfly.'

'So has my snail,' cried the old man.

Then they started to laugh. 'It is the very same snail!' they

said. 'What shall we do?'

The old man had an idea. 'Well,' he said, 'the little snail seems to enjoy my cabbages just as much as he enjoys your lettuces. I will grow a row of cabbages specially for him, if you will grow a row of lettuces for him too.'

'Oh, I'm sure he would like that!' laughed the old woman. 'And every week we will meet in the lane and hand him over. He will eat cabbage one week and lettuce the next.'

The snail was delighted with the arrangement. It isn't every snail who has two homes, and he used to look forward to his trip down the lane every week.

As for the old man and the old woman, they became the very best of friends. And all because of the little snail who would not go away.

Puss in Boots

Charles Perrault

ONCE UPON A TIME there was a miller who had three sons. When he died, he left behind only his mill, his donkey and his cat. His eldest son had the mill, the second son had the donkey and the youngest son had the cat.

The youngest son was very disappointed. 'My brothers,' he said, 'can make a living by working together, for one can grind corn and the other can carry it to market on the donkey. But I have nothing but a cat and I shall soon die of hunger.'

But the cat heard his master and said, 'Don't be downhearted. Just buy me a pair of boots and a bag and you will soon see that I am more valuable than the mill or the donkey.'

The cat's master agreed to do this and spent his last pennies on a splendid pair of boots and a strong bag for the cat.

The cat was full of joy when he put on the fine boots. 'Now I am Puss in Boots,' he cried and, taking the bag, he put some bran and lettuce into it. Then he went into a field where there were a great number of rabbits and stretched himself out as if he were dead, with the strings of the bag between his paws. He waited for a silly young rabbit to come along and eat the bran and lettuce in the bag.

Almost at once he got what he wanted. A young rabbit jumped into the bag and Puss pulled the drawstrings shut.

Delighted at his luck, he set off for the palace and asked to see the king. The servants were astonished to see a cat in boots but they brought him to the king's throne anyway.

Bowing low to the king, he said: 'Your Majesty, my master, the Marquis of Carabas, sends you this rabbit as a present.'

'Tell your master,' said the king, 'that I thank him very

much for his kind present.'

Next day, the cat hid himself in a cornfield and caught two pigeons in his bag. He went again to the king and presented them as a gift from his master, the Marquis of Carabas.

The king was pleased with the pigeons and ordered some money to be given to the cat.

The cat went on giving the king presents in the name of his master for several weeks.

Now the king had a very beautiful daughter who was his only child. One day Puss heard that the king and his daughter were going out in their carriage along the road by the river.

He quickly ran back to his master and told him to bathe in the river and ask no questions.

Puss's master did as he was told and when he was in the

river, Puss hid his old clothes.

Before long, the king's carriage came by and the cat began to shout: 'Help! Help! My master, the Marquis of Carabas, is drowning!'

The king, hearing the cries and recognizing the cat who had brought him presents, sent his guards to help.

While they were pulling the Marquis of Carabas out of the river, the cat explained that his master's clothes had been stolen by thieves while he was bathing so, though he was saved, he had no clothes to put on.

The king at once ordered a magnificent outfit to be brought for the Marquis of Carabas and when he was dressed and came to the door of the king's carriage, the princess fell in love with him at once.

The quick-thinking cat ran ahead of the carriage and asked the people he passed working in the fields to say that the land belonged to the Marquis of Carabas. Soon the king came by and when he asked whose land he was passing through, the reply always came that the land belonged to the Marquis of

Carabas. The king thought that the cat's master was very wealthy.

At last, Puss arrived at a huge castle where an ogre lived who was also a magician. This ogre was the richest person in the land, for he owned all of the land which the king now thought belonged to the Marquis of Carabas. Puss told the ogre that he had heard he was a great magician. 'I have been told,' said Puss, 'that you can change yourself into any shape you choose. Is this true?'

'Indeed it is,' roared the ogre and, to prove his point, he turned into a lion. Puss was very scared but he said to the ogre, 'You are wonderfully clever but I suppose you can only take the shape of big and strong creatures like yourself and you would not be able to turn yourself into a little mouse.'

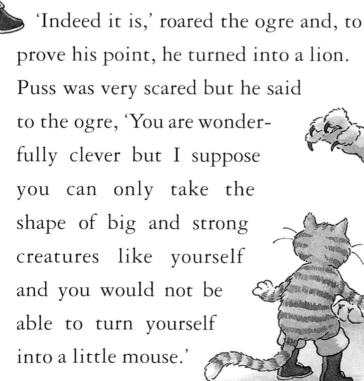

'Oh yes I can,' replied the ogre and he changed himself into a mouse and ran across the floor.

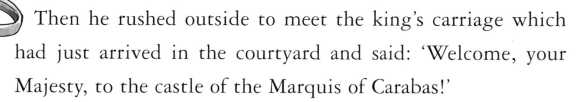

Quick as a flash, Puss sprang forward and gobbled up the mouse before it could turn back into the ogre.

Then he rushed outside to meet the king's carriage which had just arrived in the courtyard and said: 'Welcome, your Majesty, to the castle of the Marquis of Carabas!'

The king was surprised and delighted at the grandeur of the castle and asked to be shown around. And so the miller's son gave his arm to the princess and they all wandered in and sat down to a banquet that the ogre had prepared for his friends.

The king gave his daughter's hand in marriage to the handsome young Marquis, and Puss in Boots became a lord and never had to hunt mice again.

THE STRANGE BIRD

Adèle Geras

IT STARTED OFF as quite an ordinary day in the jungle. The
birds were singing their morning songs. Momma Elephant
and her children were coming home from brushing their tusks
beside the river.

Tiger and his wife were having breakfast.
Giraffe was just setting out to visit
Leopard when he noticed a strange bird
sitting on a branch of the jacaranda tree.

'I've never seen a bird like that
before,' said Giraffe. 'It's shiny. Birds

aren't supposed to be shiny, are they, Momma Elephant?'

'Certainly not,' said Momma Elephant, peering up at the tree. 'It looks dangerous to me, with that sharp beak. Little Six, go and fetch Tiger and Leopard here at once. We should decide what's to be done about it.'

Little Six was back very quickly, with Tiger and his wife and Leopard huffing and puffing anxiously behind her.

Tiger whispered, 'I expect it's foreign. I've certainly never seen a bird like that in this jungle. Perhaps we should all approach it together. Can't be too careful, you know. Got to find out if it's friendly.'

Leopard said, 'I don't like the way the sunlight bounces off its back. It dazzles you just to look at it.'

'If everybody's here,' said Momma Elephant, 'we should

gather round it together. It wouldn't dare to attack so many of us. Come along, all of you, form a straight line behind me.'

All the animals grouped together according to size, and the birds and butterflies flew along overhead.

The strange bird did not move, but sat quietly on its branch.

'Excuse me,' said Momma Elephant, 'but we would like to know who you are and where you come from and especially whether you are friendly. We've never seen a bird quite like you before and we're all a little worried.'

The strange bird spoke, 'Please do not worry. I am a Mirror Bird and I come from Mirror Bird Mountain, which lies across the ocean. I have heard that this is a very pleasant jungle, so I have come to see it for myself. I mean you no harm.'

'That's all very well,' said Leopard, 'but what is a mirror?'

'A mirror,' said the strange bird, 'is a glass in which you can see yourself. Come closer.'

Gingerly, the animals made a circle around the tree. The Mirror Bird flew down to the lowest branch and one by one the animals looked into the thousands of mirrors that sparkled on its breast and its wings.

'Goodness,' said Giraffe, 'is that really me? My neck does stretch on and on, doesn't it?'

Tiger said to his wife, 'Our stripes are really rather handsome, don't you think?'

'See how long and coiled I am!' said Snake. 'I never realized.'

'I am far more wrinkled than I thought. Perhaps I shouldn't frown so much,' sighed Momma Elephant. 'But my ears are still magnificent.'

'We are even prettier than we thought we were,' said the butterflies.

'We think we're even prettier than you are,' said the birds.

Leopard looked into the mirror. 'I think I look rather tired. I shall take a small snooze. Thank you, Mirror Bird.'

'It seems to me,' said Momma Elephant, 'that you are going

to be a great help to everyone. You can show us all what we are like, and teach us things about ourselves that we didn't know before. You're most welcome in our jungle.'

All the animals were now very eager to show the Mirror Bird around the jungle.

'You are very beautiful,' sang the birds as they flew with the Mirror Bird over the twisting, silver river that ran through the jungle. 'Quite different from us, of course, but very beautiful.'

'We must apologize,' said Tiger, offering the Mirror Bird some fruit as they visited his home, 'if we frightened you, all marching up to you like that. But you frightened us too, you know! We'd be honoured if you would like to stay in our jungle.'

'Can my friends come too?' asked the Mirror Bird.

'Of course,' said Giraffe, as they walked around his tall house, 'there's plenty of room for everyone here.'

'Certainly there is,' said Momma Elephant, as she hurried to find her guest a perch. 'I'm sorry we were rude to you at first. You are to make yourself completely at home.'

She pushed her children into a line.

'Go and see that your ears are tidily placed. There's no excuse for looking untidy now we have the Mirror Bird with us,' she smiled.

The little elephants did as they were told, and then the Mirror Bird flew to the top of the jacaranda tree and started building her nest.

THE WAY OUT

Joyce Dunbar

THOMPSON WAS A LONG-HAIRED hamster. He was very clean and very curious. He belonged to a boy called Luke. Thompson's cage was in Luke's bedroom. It was a good-sized cage, with an upstairs and a downstairs. It had a newspaper nest inside a sleeping compartment, drinking water in a bottle on the side, a wheel and two ladders.

Thompson slept all day, but when night time came he was up and about. He ran around his cage, up and down his ladders, round and round in his wheel. But that wasn't enough. Thompson wanted to find the way out.

One night, after Luke had gone to bed, Thompson saw that his cage door was open! Thompson stayed still for a minute, sat on his hind legs, smartened up his whiskers and listened. He could feel the big room all around him!

He scrambled through the open door and toppled on to the bedroom floor. Across the carpet he scuttled, under the bed, into the cupboard, along the shelves, in and out of shoes, in between Luke's toys. But that still wasn't enough.

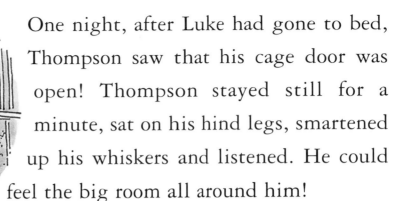

Thompson wanted to find the way out.

So he gnawed at the skirting board and scraped at the floorboards. He sniffed at the gap by the door, then managed to squeeze his way through. Thompson stayed still for a moment, pricked up his ears and listened. He could feel the big house all around him!

Through the bedrooms he ran, in and out of the bathroom, before scrambling all the way downstairs. He went into the

living room, behind the sofa, in and out of drawers, under the door into the kitchen. Even so, that wasn't enough.

Thompson wanted to find the way out.

Then he smelt something through the cat-flap in the door. Fresh air! He flipped through on to the path outside. There he stayed still for a moment, took a deep breath and listened. He could feel the big town all around him!

Across the garden he ran, through the gate, all along the street, past the shops and schools, until he reached the middle of the town. Even so, that wasn't enough.

Thompson wanted to find the way out.

Then he saw a bus waiting at the bus-stop. Thompson stayed still for a moment, cocked his head on one side and listened. He could sense the big country all around him!

So he stowed away on the bus and went through villages, towns and cities. He hopped on and off trains which took him up and down dale. He ran through forests and over fields until he came to the edge of the land. Yet still that wasn't enough.

Thompson wanted to find the way out. Then he saw the wide open sea. Thompson sat still for a moment, polished his nose with his paws and listened. He could feel the great world all around him!

So he stowed away on a ship, to the North Pole and the South Pole. And he stowed away on aeroplanes to the East and to the West. Soon he had been right around the world! But it just wasn't enough.

Thompson wanted to find the way out.

He looked up at the great empty sky. Thompson sat still for a moment, heaved a big sigh and listened. He could feel outer space all above him!

So he stowed away on a rocket to the moon. He ran all around the moon, in and out of craters. Then he jumped on to a shooting star which took him to the edge of the universe.

He peeped over the edge of the universe. He saw an endless big black hole!

E-E-E-K!

Thompson had had quite enough. He wanted to find the way home.

Thompson sat still for a moment, stood on his hind legs and suddenly felt very dizzy. He covered his eyes with his paws and fell into the big black hole.

Down and down he went, very fast and far, until he landed with a very soft bump.

Thompson uncovered his eyes. He was back inside Luke's room.

'Where have you been?' cried Luke. 'I've been looking everywhere for you!' Luke picked him up and stroked him and put him back inside his cage, with an upstairs and a downstairs and a wheel and two ladders.

Thompson sat still for a moment, then he had some biscuit for breakfast and a drink from his bottle. He smoothed down his fur and curled up in his newspaper nest.

How cosy and sleepy he felt! How very safe and sound!

THE WONDERFUL SMELL

from
CYRIL'S CAT
AND THE BIG SURPRISE

Shoo Rayner

CYRIL'S CAT CHARLIE was bored. He had been bored for two or three days. Cyril was worried about him. At supper time Charlie came into the kitchen and looked at his food.

Not that tinned stuff again, he thought. I'm so bored with the tinned stuff. Then he swished his tail and went outside to sit in the drizzling rain.

Cyril watched him through the kitchen window. 'I wonder what the matter is,' he said to himself. 'Maybe he doesn't like

his food. I'll see if I can get something nice for him tomorrow.'

When Cyril got up the next morning, Charlie still hadn't touched his supper. Cyril gave him a saucer of cream but Charlie didn't even try it. Instead he dragged himself through the cat-flap and found a puddle to lie in.

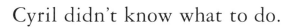

Cyril didn't know what to do.

Charlie just lay in the puddle with his eyes shut. He didn't even twitch when a fly landed on his whiskers. He heard Cyril close the gate behind him, as he went off to the shops, but he wasn't interested. He was bored and fed up and that was all there was to it!

Then Charlie's nose began to twitch. He could smell something just . . . well . . . wonderful, and it seemed to come from over the fence.

Charlie forgot that he was bored and went off to investigate.

He squeezed through a hole in the fence and found Hercules, the cat who lived next door, keeping a watch on the bird table. 'Can you smell anything?' asked Charlie.

Hercules lifted his nose high into the air and sniffed, first this way then that. 'MMMMMM!' he sighed. 'I can smell it all right. I think it's coming from over there.'

The two cats walked to the bottom of the garden. They had one thing on their minds.

Where was that wonderful smell coming from? They crossed six gardens and two roads. The scent was getting stronger.

They stopped in front of an old, rusty dustbin that someone had left on the pavement. This was where the wonderful smell was coming from.

The lid wasn't on properly so they climbed in. There was a lot of other rubbish, but they soon found what they were looking for.

Wrapped in a sheet of soggy newspaper were the leftovers of a poached salmon. It was yummy, and they got to work on it as if they hadn't eaten for days, which, in Charlie's case, was true.

They were having such a good time that they didn't notice the dust-cart moving slowly down the street. They didn't notice until they were hurled into the back of the dust-cart!

They landed upside down in a heap of coffee grounds and potato peelings.

They were very surprised and they were trapped! The rubbish cruncher was right behind them. A wall of rubbish was in front of them. They climbed up and up the rubbish pile until they found a hiding place right at the top. It was dark and smelly. Charlie and Hercules were not very happy.

They stayed there while the dust-cart did its rounds, collecting the rubbish. It seemed a very long time before they were tossed out of their hiding place into the bright daylight and on to the mountain of rubbish at the tip.

The driver of the dust-cart heard an odd noise when he emptied out the rubbish. He thought it sounded like a pair of unhappy cats.

When he went to the back of the truck he saw it *was* a pair of unhappy cats! Charlie and Hercules looked very sorry for themselves. They smelled a bit too!

The driver knew Charlie quite well; he always said hello to him when they came round

each week. He picked up the cats, put them in the cab and gave them a lift home.

'Well!' said Charlie. 'That was too much of an adventure for me. I never want to see poached salmon again.' Hercules agreed. They both went home to see if they had been missed.

Cyril had been very worried about Charlie and was very happy when he came through the cat-flap. He was so pleased he didn't even notice that Charlie smelled like a rubbish tip!

'Oh, Charlie,' Cyril sighed, 'you had me so worried. I'm glad you are home. Look, I've got something special for your supper.' He bent down and put a bowl in front of Charlie. 'I got it specially,' he continued, 'because you haven't eaten properly for days. It's a little bit of poached salmon!'

THE ELEPHANT'S PICNIC

Richard Hughes

ELEPHANTS ARE GENERALLY clever animals, but there was once an elephant who was very silly; and his great friend was a kangaroo. Now, kangaroos are not often clever animals, and this one certainly was not, so she and the elephant got on very well together.

One day they thought they would like to go off for a picnic by themselves. But they did not know anything about picnics, and had not the faintest idea of what to do to get ready.

'What do you do on a picnic?' the elephant asked a child he knew.

'Oh, we collect wood and make a fire, and then we boil the kettle,' said the child.

'What do you boil the kettle for?' said the elephant in surprise.

'Why, for tea, of course,' said the child in a snapping sort of way; so the elephant did not like to ask any more questions. But he went and told the kangaroo, and they collected together all the things they thought they would need.

When they got to the place where they were going to have their picnic, the kangaroo said that she would collect the wood because she had got a pouch to carry it back in. A kangaroo's pouch, of course, is very small; so the kangaroo careful-ly chose the smallest twigs she could find, and only about five or six of those. In fact, it took a lot of hopping to find any sticks small enough to go in her pouch at all; and it was a long time before she came back. But silly though the elephant was, he soon saw those sticks would not be enough for a fire.

'Now *I* will go off and get some wood,' he said.

His ideas of getting wood were very different. Instead of taking little twigs he pushed down whole trees with his forehead, and staggered back to the picnic-place with them rolled up in his trunk.

Then the kangaroo struck a match, and they lit a bonfire made of whole trees. The blaze, of course, was enormous, and the fire so hot that for a long time they could not get near it; and it was not until it began to die down a bit that they were able to get near enough to cook anything.

'Now let's boil the kettle,' said the elephant. Amongst the things he had brought was a brightly shining copper kettle and a very large black iron saucepan.

The elephant filled the saucepan with water.

'What are you doing that for?' said the kangaroo.

'To boil the kettle in, you silly,' said the elephant. So he popped the kettle in the saucepan of water, and put the saucepan on the fire; for he thought that you boil a kettle in the same sort of way you boil an egg, or boil a cabbage! And the kangaroo, of course, did not know any better.

So they boiled and boiled the kettle, and every now and then they prodded it with a stick.

'It doesn't seem to be getting tender,' said the elephant sadly, 'and I am sure we can't eat it for tea until it does.'

So then away he went and got more wood for the fire; and still the saucepan boiled and boiled, and still the kettle remained as hard as ever.

It was getting late now, almost dark.

'I am afraid it won't be ready for tea,' said the kangaroo. 'I am afraid we shall have to spend the night here. I wish we had got something with us to sleep in.'

'Haven't you?' said the elephant. 'You mean to say you didn't pack before you came away?'

'No,' said the kangaroo. 'What should I have packed, anyway?'

'Why, your trunk, of course,' said the elephant. 'That is what people pack.'

'But I haven't got a trunk,' said the kangaroo.

'Well, I have,' said the elephant, 'and I've packed it. Kindly pass the pepper; I want to unpack!'

So then the kangaroo passed the elephant the pepper, and the elephant took a good sniff. Then he gave a most enormous sneeze, and everything he had packed in his trunk shot out of it – toothbrush, spare socks, gym shoes, a comb, a bag of bull's-eyes, his pyjamas, and his suit.

So then the elephant put on his pyjamas and lay down to sleep; but the kangaroo had no pyjamas, and so, of course, she could not possibly sleep.

'All right,' she said to the elephant, 'you sleep and I will sit up and keep the fire going.'

So all night the kangaroo kept the fire blazing brightly and the kettle boiling merrily in the saucepan.

When the next morning came the elephant woke up.

'Now,' he said, 'let's have our breakfast.'

So they took the kettle out of the saucepan; and what do you think? *It was boiled as tender as tender could be!* So they cut it fairly in half and shared it between them, and ate it for their breakfast; and both agreed they had never had so good a breakfast in their lives.

CHICKEN LICKEN

Traditional

ONE DAY, WHEN Chicken Licken was in the wood, an acorn fell from a tree on to his poor bald head.

'Oh dear,' thought Chicken Licken. 'The sky is falling! I must go and tell the king.'

So he left the wood and headed for the king's palace. On the way there he met Hen Len.

'Well, Hen Len,' he said, 'where are you going?'

'I'm going to the wood,' said Hen Len.

'Oh, don't go there,' said Chicken Licken, 'for I was there and the sky fell on my poor bald head and I'm going to tell the king.'

'Can I come with you?' asked Hen Len.

'Certainly,' said Chicken Licken.

So they both went off together to tell the king the sky was falling.

As they travelled along, they met Cock Lock. 'Well, Cock Lock,' said Hen Len, 'where are you going?'

'I'm going to the wood,' said Cock Lock.

'Oh, Cock Lock, don't go there,' said Hen Len, 'for Chicken Licken was there and the sky fell on his poor bald head and we're going to tell the king.'

'May I come with you?' said Cock Lock.

'Certainly,' said Chicken Licken.

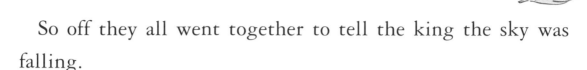

So off they all went together to tell the king the sky was falling.

As they travelled onwards, they met Duck Luck. 'Well, Duck Luck,' said Cock Lock, 'where are you going?'

'I'm going to the wood,' said Duck Luck.

'Oh, Duck Luck, don't go there,' said Cock Lock, 'for Chicken Licken was there and the sky fell on his poor bald head and we're going to tell the king.'

'May I come with you?' said Duck Luck.

'Of course,' said Chicken Licken, and so off they all went together to tell the king the sky was falling.

Before long they met Drake Lake. 'Well, Drake Lake,' said Duck Luck, 'where are you going?'

'I'm going to the wood,' said Drake Lake.

'Oh, Drake Lake, don't go there,' said Duck Luck, 'for Chicken Licken was there and the sky fell on his poor bald head and we're going to tell the king.'

'May I come with you?' asked Drake Lake.

'Of course,' said Chicken Licken, and off they all went together to tell the king the sky was falling.

On they travelled until they met Goose Loose. 'Well, Goose Loose,' said Drake Lake, 'where are you going?'

'I'm going to the wood,' said Goose Loose.

'Oh, Goose Loose, don't go there,' said Drake Lake, 'for Chicken Licken was there and the sky fell on his poor bald head and we're going to tell the king.'

'May I come with you?' said Goose Loose.

'Certainly,' said Chicken Licken, and off they all went together to tell the king the sky was falling.

On their way they met Turkey Lurkey. 'Well, Turkey Lurkey,' said Goose Loose, 'where are you going?'

'I'm going to the wood,' said Turkey Lurkey.

'Oh, Turkey Lurkey, don't go there,' said Goose Loose, 'for Chicken Licken was there and the sky fell on his poor bald head and we're off to tell the king.'

'May I come with you?' said Turkey Lurkey.

'Of course,' said Chicken Licken, and off they all went to tell the king that the sky was falling.

A little while later they met Fox Lox. And Fox Lox said, 'Where are you going?'

'Chicken Licken was in the wood and the sky fell on his

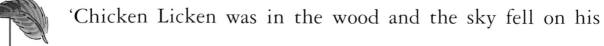

poor bald head,' said all the birds together, 'and we're going to tell the king.'

'Come with me,' said Fox Lox, 'and I will show you the way to the palace. The king will be delighted to see you.'

They all followed Fox Lox until they came to a dark, dark hole in the edge of the hillside. 'This is the way to the king's palace,' said Fox Lox. So in went Chicken Licken, Hen Len, Cock Lock, Duck Luck, Drake Lake, Goose Loose and Turkey Lurkey, one after the other. But this was not the way to the king's palace, it was Fox Lox's den. And in no time at all Fox Lox had gobbled up every one of them, so they never saw the king to tell him that the sky was falling.

A FISH OF THE WORLD

Terry Jones

A HERRING ONCE DECIDED to swim right round the world. 'I'm tired of the North Sea,' he said. 'I want to find out what else there is in the world.'

So he swam off south into the deep Atlantic. He swam and he swam far far away from the seas he knew, through the warm waters of the equator and on down into the South Atlantic. And all the time he saw

many strange and wonderful fish that he had never seen before. Once he was nearly eaten by a shark, and once he was nearly electrocuted by an electric eel, and once he was nearly stung by a sting-ray. But he swam on and on, round the tip of Africa and into the

Indian Ocean. And he passed by devilfish and sailfish and saw-fish and swordfish and bluefish and blackfish and mudfish and sunfish, and he was amazed by the different shapes and sizes and colours.

On he swam, into the Java Sea, and he saw fish that leapt out of the water and fish that lived on the bottom of the sea and fish that could walk on their fins. And on he swam,

through the Coral Sea, where the shells of millions and millions of tiny creatures had turned to rock and stood as big as mountains. But still he swam on, into the wide Pacific. He swam over the deepest parts of the ocean where the water is so deep that it is inky black at the bottom, and the fish carry lanterns over their heads, and some have lights on their tails. And through the Pacific he swam, and then he turned north and headed up to the cold Siberian Sea, where huge white icebergs sailed past him like mighty ships. And still he swam on and on and into the frozen Arctic Ocean, where the sea is forever covered in ice. And on he went, past Greenland and Iceland, and finally he swam home into his own North Sea.

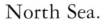

All his friends and relations gathered round and made a great fuss of him. They had a big feast and offered him the very best food they could find. But the herring just yawned and said: 'I've swum round the entire world. I have seen everything there is to see, and I have eaten more exotic and wonderful dishes than you could possibly imagine.' And he refused to eat anything.

Then his friends and relations begged him to come home and live with them, but he refused. 'I've been everywhere there is, and that old rock is too dull and small for me.' And he went

off and lived on his own.

And when the breeding season came, he refused to join in the spawning, saying: 'I've swum round the entire world, and now I know how many fish there are in the world, I can't be interested in herrings any more.'

Eventually, one of the oldest of the herrings swam up to him, and said: 'Listen. If you don't spawn with us, some herrings' eggs will go unfertilized and will not turn into healthy young herring. If you don't live with your family, you'll make them sad. And if you don't eat, you'll die.'

But the herring said: 'I don't mind. I've been everywhere there is to go, I've seen everything there is to see, and now I know everything there is to know.'

The old fish shook his head. 'No one has ever seen everything there is to see,'

he said, 'nor known everything there is to know.'

'Look,' said the herring, 'I've swum through the North Sea, the Atlantic Ocean, the Indian Ocean, the Java Sea, the Coral Sea, the great Pacific Ocean, the Siberian Sea and the frozen Arctic. Tell me, what else is there for me to see or know?'

'I don't know,' said the old herring, 'but there may be something.'

Well, just then, a fishing-boat came by, and all the herrings were caught in a net and taken to market that very day. And a man bought the herring, and ate it for his supper.

And he never knew that it had swum right round the world, and had seen everything there was to see, and knew everything there was to know.

THE LION WHO COULDN'T ROAR

Hilda Carson

ONCE THERE WAS a little lion who lived in the forest with his father and mother.

When Father Lion had been out hunting, and roared to let Mother Lion know he was coming home, you could hear him all over the forest. And when Mother Lion roared back, you could hear *her* all over the forest. But the little lion had just a little voice.

'Never mind,' said Mother Lion. 'As you grow bigger, your voice will grow bigger, too.'

But it didn't.

One day Uncle Lion came to visit.

'We are glad to see you,' roared Mother Lion.

'Where have you been all this time?' roared Father Lion.

'Been on my summer holiday hunting trip,' roared Uncle Lion. 'And how are you, young fellow?'

'Very well, thank you,' said the little lion in his little voice.

'Bless my soul!' said Uncle Lion. 'What's the matter? Lost your voice?'

'Not all of my voice,' said the little lion. 'Just my roar.'

'High time you found it!' said Uncle Lion.

The little lion sat down and thought about what Uncle Lion had said, and after a while, when the grown-ups were busy talking, he went off into the forest, all by himself.

He saw some monkeys playing in the branches of a tall tree.

'Excuse me, please,' said the little lion politely, 'I've lost my voice. Not all of my voice, just my roar. Do you know where I might find it?'

The monkeys laughed till they almost fell out of the tree.

'Look at the lion without a roar!' they shouted. 'Listen to his little voice! Say something more, lion!' And they swung upside down from the branches, and threw twigs and leaves down on him.

'I think you're very rude,' said the little lion in his little voice, and he went away, out of the trees and down to the river.

At the edge of the river he found Mr Hippopotamus dozing in a nice warm squishy mud bath.

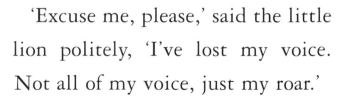

'Excuse me, please,' said the little lion politely, 'I've lost my voice. Not all of my voice, just my roar.'

Mr Hippopotamus opened one eye. 'And a good thing, too,' he said. 'There's too much noise around here.'

'Do you know where I might find it?' asked the little lion.

'Certainly not,' said Mr Hippopotamus, 'and if I did, I wouldn't tell you.' And he went to sleep again.

The little lion went on through the forest till he found a pretty little green snake curled up on top of a rock.

'Excuse me, please,' he said politely, 'I've lost my voice. Not all of my voice, just my roar. Do you know where I might find it?'

The little snake uncurled herself slowly.

'Yes-s-s,' she said at last. 'I think I know the very place where you might find your roar, but it's in a very dangerous-s-s part of the forest.'

'I don't mind,' said the little lion bravely.

'Follow me, then,' said the snake. 'This-s-s way.'

And she slipped down from the rock and slid away among the trees so fast that the little lion had to run to keep up with her.

Soon they came to a part of the forest where the little lion had never been before. The trees were very tall and very close together, so that it was dark underneath them, and the bushes were so thick that there was no path through them.

'This-s-s is the place,' said the little snake, and she slid into the bushes and disappeared.

'Come back!' said the little lion. 'Don't leave me alone here!'

But the little green snake didn't come back.

'Mother!' said the little lion in his little voice. 'Mother! I don't know where I am! I think I'm lost!'

But of course Mother Lion couldn't hear him.

The little lion sat down and looked round him. It was very dark and very lonely, and he was very frightened.

So he cried. And he howled. And he ROARED. And from far away in the forest Mother Lion roared back, 'I'm here, my little son! I'm coming!'

The little green snake slid out from under the bushes where she had been hiding all the time.

'I'm s-s-sorry I s-s-scared you,' she said, 'but I thought you'd find your roar if you ever *really* needed it.' And she disappeared again.

Then the three big lions came bounding through the forest to where the little lion was. Father Lion hugged him, and Mother Lion kissed him, and Uncle Lion said, 'Bless my soul, with a roar like that you should grow up to be the biggest lion in the forest.'

And they all went home together.

TORTOISE LONGS TO FLY

Hiawyn Oram

Tortoise was lying in the sun when he heard the other animals talking about him in the bushes.

'Tortoise is so slow and plain,' he heard, 'it's hard to keep a straight face watching him.'

It upset Tortoise dreadfully. He felt his pride hurt like soft skin by sharp thorns. He thought of crawling into a dark cave and staying there for a long time. Then he had a better idea and went to find Osprey.

'Good morning, Tortoise! How are you, old chap?'

Osprey was so great and strong he never felt the need to

look down on others.

'Very well,' Tortoise lied.

'And what can I do for you?' said Osprey.

'You can come to dinner,' said Tortoise.

'What a delightful idea,' said Osprey. 'I couldn't be more pleased to accept.'

So that evening Osprey joined Tortoise and his wife for dinner. And what a feast it was. Mrs Tortoise had outdone herself.

'Why,' said Osprey, 'this is quite the best dinner I've ever eaten. And as for these bananas! Where do you get them?'

'Aha,' said Tortoise. 'That would be telling! But since you have enjoyed everything so much you must come again – and often.'

'I'd be honoured,' said Osprey and meant it.

And after that the great Osprey regularly went to dinner with the Tortoises. And, as Tortoise had planned, the other animals noticed and were most impressed.

'Well, he can't be that slow and plain, if the great and good Osprey spends so much time with him,' they marvelled.

And Tortoise heard them and felt positively cheerful about himself again. But not for long. Spiteful, sharp-tongued Chameleon made sure of that.

'So when will your great friend Osprey be inviting you to dinner in his nest?' he said.

'Oh, he has,' said Tortoise. 'He asks me all the time. But so far I've been too busy to accept.'

'Really?' said Chameleon cruelly. 'Or just unable to get there? Unless of course you are learning to fly!'

And once again Tortoise felt as if he had been stuck with thorns.

'If only I could fly,' he muttered angrily, 'that would show 'em. And maybe, just maybe, I will!'

With a plan forming by the second, he went to find his wife

and engage her help.

First, as instructed, she invited Osprey to dinner. Next, with some difficulty, but as instructed, she wrapped Tortoise in a bundle of banana leaves.

Then, when Osprey arrived for dinner, she said, 'Oh, Osprey, Tortoise has had to make a sudden visit to see his sick mother. But by way of apology, he asks you to accept this bunch of bananas – all wrapped up so they won't bruise on your way home.'

And while Osprey was sorry about Tortoise's sick mother he was very pleased about the bananas.

He picked up the bundle and flew off towards his nest thinking of nothing but a big banana feast.

While Tortoise, inside the bundle, was thinking of

nothing but how it would wipe the smile off the others' faces when they found he had flown to Osprey's for dinner!

But unfortunately Tortoise's happy thoughts were quickly overcome by some very strange feelings: dizziness, panic, sickness and fear.

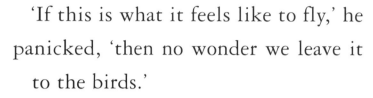

'If this is what it feels like to fly,' he panicked, 'then no wonder we leave it to the birds.'

He bore it as long as he could – which wasn't long. 'Hey, Osprey!' he soon yelled. 'There's been a terrible mistake. Please, please, PUT ME DOWN!'

And Osprey, terrified at the idea of carrying a bunch of speaking bananas, opened his beak and gave a terrific squawk. And down went the bundle – Tortoise and all.

KER-WHACKKK!

'Oh my goodness!' Mrs Tortoise cried when he eventually limped home. 'What has Osprey done to you?'

'Dropped me!' Tortoise almost wept. 'From a great height.

Right on my shell. And I'm sure it's terribly cracked.'

'Well,' Mrs Tortoise blushed. 'Cracked it certainly is. All over. In a criss-crossy sort of way. But do you know, I think Osprey may have done you a favour. It's a great improvement.'

And that was the opinion of all.

'Very elegant, so interesting, very smart indeed!' the other animals raved.

Even Chameleon had to admit that in his new patterned shell there was nothing plain about Tortoise.

And since Tortoise was the first tortoise, to this day there are those who insist that that's how the criss-cross patterned beauty of tortoise-shell was born.

THE MOUSE'S BRIDEGROOM

*A story from Burma
retold by Barbara Ker Wilson*

A FAMILY OF MICE once lived in a farmhouse: father, mother and daughter. The two fond parents thought their daughter was the most beautiful mouse in the world, with her smooth brown coat, her long pink tail and her delicate whiskers.

Another mouse, a bachelor, lived in the cattleshed in the farmyard. He was young and handsome and he wanted to marry the beautiful Miss Mouse. But her parents did not consider him good enough for their daughter. They wanted her to marry the most powerful being on earth. So they told young Mister Mouse to go away.

What did Miss Mouse herself feel about this? She was very sad, for she had fallen in love with the young mouse from the cattleshed. Her brown coat lost its shine, and her delicate whiskers drooped.

Her parents, however, took no notice. Instead, they set out to find a bridegroom worthy of their daughter.

'Surely the Sun is the most powerful being of all,' said Father Mouse. 'He shines down upon the earth and ripens the corn in the fields. Let us ask the Sun to marry our daughter.'

So the two parent mice stood in the cornfield and asked the bright yellow Sun if he would marry their daughter. They were delighted when the Sun readily agreed to their proposal.

But no sooner had he said 'yes' than Mother Mouse felt a qualm of doubt. 'Ask him if he is really the most powerful being of all,'

she urged Father Mouse.

So Father Mouse asked the Sun, 'Are you really the most powerful being of all?'

'No,' answered the Sun. 'The Rain is more powerful than I am. For when a Rain Cloud covers the sky, I am blotted out completely.'

Even as he spoke, a great black Rain Cloud drifted across the Sun's face, hiding him from sight.

'In that case, I am very sorry, but you may not marry our daughter after all!' called Father Mouse, just before the Sun disappeared from view.

Then he addressed the Rain Cloud. 'Tell me, Rain Cloud, are you in fact the most powerful being of all?'

The Rain Cloud scowled down at the two mice in the cornfield. 'No, I am not,' he replied. 'The Wind is more powerful than I am. For when the Wind blows, I am torn to shreds and scattered across the sky.'

'In that case, I am afraid you may not marry our daughter

either,' said Father Mouse.

At that moment, the Wind began to blow. He swept across the sky, scattering the great black Rain Cloud in pieces.

'Oh, Wind!' shouted Father Mouse. 'Is it true that you are the most powerful being of all?'

'No, not I!' blustered the Wind. 'Do you see that big grey Stone in the corner of the field? It is more powerful than I am. I cannot move it, however hard I blow.'

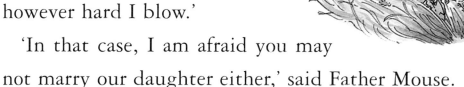

'In that case, I am afraid you may not marry our daughter either,' said Father Mouse.

Now the two mice went over to the big grey Stone that stood in one corner of the field.

'Are you the most powerful being of all?' Father Mouse asked the Stone.

'No, indeed,' answered the Stone. 'The red Bull is more powerful than I am. Every day he comes to sharpen his horns against my surface, breaking off splinters of rock as he does so.'

'In that case, I am afraid you may not marry our daughter either,' said Father Mouse.

Next the two mice went to interview the red Bull, who stood tethered in his stall in the cattleshed.

'I think,' said Father Mouse, 'that you must be the most powerful being of all, and I have come to offer you my daughter.'

'You are wrong!' roared the Bull. 'This Rope that tethers me is more powerful than I am.'

'Oh,' said Father Mouse. 'In that case, I am afraid you may not marry our daughter after all.'

Now Mother Mouse spoke to the strong Rope that tethered the Bull. 'So you are the most powerful being of all!' she squeaked. 'Will you marry our daughter?'

'Much as I should like to marry your daughter,' replied the Rope, 'I must admit that there is one being even more powerful than I am, and that is the young Mouse who lives in this cattleshed. Every night, as the Bull stands tethered in his stall, this Mouse comes to gnaw at me with his sharp teeth. In time he will gnaw right through me, and I will break.'

'Well,' said Father Mouse. And, 'Well, well!' exclaimed Mother Mouse. They looked at each other shamefacedly. Then they sought out the handsome young bachelor Mouse who lived in the cattleshed, and begged him to marry their daughter after all.

Young Mister Mouse was very surprised, and quite over-joyed. As for Miss Mouse, when she heard the good news that she was to marry the bridegroom of her own choice after all, her coat at once regained its shine, and she preened her delicate whiskers prettily. So the two mice were married and lived happily ever after.

THE THREE BEARS

Traditional

ONCE UPON A TIME there were three bears who lived together in the wood. One of them was a little bear, one was a middle-sized bear and the third was a great big bear. They each had a bowl for their porridge – a little bowl for the little bear, a middle-sized bowl for the middle-sized bear and a great big bowl for the great big bear. And they

each had a chair to sit on – a little chair for the little bear, a middle-sized chair for the middle-sized bear and a great big chair for the great big bear. And they each had a bed to sleep in – a little bed for the little bear, a middle-sized bed for the middle-sized bear and a great big bed for the great big bear.

One day, after they had made the porridge for their break-fast and poured it into their bowls, they walked out in the woods while the porridge was cooling. A little girl named Goldilocks passed by the house and looked in at the window. And then she looked in at the keyhole and when she saw that there was no one home, she lifted the latch on the door.

The door was not locked because the

bears were good bears who never did anyone any harm and never thought that anyone would harm them. So Goldilocks opened the door and walked in. She was very glad to see the porridge on the table, as she was hungry from walking in the woods, and so she set about helping herself.

First she tasted the porridge of the great big bear but that was too hot for her. Next she tasted the porridge of the middle-sized bear but that was too cold for her. Then she tasted the porridge of the little bear and that was neither too hot nor too cold but just right and she liked it so much that she ate it all up.

Then Goldilocks sat down on the chair of the great big bear but it was too hard for her. Next she sat down on the chair of the middle-sized bear and that was too soft for her. But when she sat in the chair of the little bear, that was neither too hard nor too soft but just right. So she sat down and there she stayed until the bottom fell out of the chair and she fell on to the floor!

Then Goldilocks went upstairs to the bedroom where the three bears slept. First she lay down upon the bed of the great big bear but that was too high for her. Next she lay down upon the bed of the middle-sized bear but that was too low for her. But when she lay down upon the bed of the little bear, it was neither too high nor too low but just right. So she covered herself up comfortably and fell fast asleep.

When the three bears thought their porridge would be cool enough for them to eat, they came home for breakfast. Now Goldilocks had left the spoon of the great big bear standing in the porridge.

'Somebody has been eating my porridge!' said the great big bear in a great rough gruff voice.

'Somebody has been eating my porridge!' said the middle-sized bear in a middle-sized voice, seeing the spoon left in the middle-sized bowl.

Then the little bear looked at its bowl and there was the

spoon standing in the bowl but the porridge was all gone.

'Somebody has been eating my porridge and has eaten it all up!' said the little bear in a little wee voice.

Upon this, the three bears, seeing that someone had come into their house and eaten up all the little bear's breakfast, began to look around them. Now Goldilocks had not put the cushion straight when she rose from the chair of the great big bear.

'Somebody has been sitting in my chair!' said the great big bear in a great rough gruff voice.

And Goldilocks had squashed down the soft cushion of the middle-sized chair.

'Somebody has been sitting in my chair!' said the middle-sized bear in a middle-sized voice.

'Somebody has been sitting in my chair and has broken it!' said the little bear in a little wee voice.

Then the three bears went to look upstairs. Goldilocks had pulled the pillow of the great big bear's bed out of its place.

'Somebody has been lying in my bed!' said the great big bear in a great rough gruff voice.

And Goldilocks had pulled the cover of the middle-sized bear's bed out of its place.

'Somebody has been lying in my bed!' said the middle-sized bear in a middle-sized voice.

But when the little wee bear came to look at its bed, there was the pillow in its place. And Golidlocks was lying on it.

'Somebody has been lying in my bed, and here she is still,' said the little bear in a little wee voice.

Goldilocks sat up and when she saw the three bears she tumbled out of the bed and ran to the window. Goldilocks jumped out of the window and ran away, and the three bears never saw her again.

ACKNOWLEDGEMENTS

The publisher gratefully acknowledges the following, for permission to reproduce copyright material in this anthology:

'Norty Boy' by Dick King-Smith from *A Narrow Squeak and Other Animal Stories* first published by Viking 1993, copyright © Fox Busters Ltd, 1993, reprinted by permission of A. P. Watt Ltd; *Fetch the Slipper* by Sheila Lavelle first published by Hamish Hamilton Ltd 1989, copyright © Sheila Lavelle, 1989, reprinted by permission of Penguin Books Ltd; *The Pocket Elephant* by Catherine Sefton first published by Hamish Hamilton Ltd 1995, copyright © Catherine Sefton, 1995, reprinted by permission of Penguin Books Ltd; *Ruby the Car-boot Rhino* by Rhiannon Powell first published by Hamish Hamilton Ltd 1995, copyright © Rhiannon Powell, 1995, reprinted by permission of Penguin Books Ltd; *Plain Jack* by K. M. Peyton first published by Hamish Hamilton Ltd 1988, copyright K. M. Peyton, 1988, reprinted by permission of Scholastic Ltd; *Sophie and the Wonderful Picture* by Kaye Umansky first published by Victor Gollancz 1993, copyright © Kaye Umansky 1993, reprinted by permission of Penguin Books Ltd; 'The Persistent Snail' by Linda Allen first published in Parents Magazine 1988, copyright © Linda Allen, 1987, reprinted by kind permission of the author c/o Rogers, Coleridge & White Ltd, 20 Powis Mews, London W11 1JN; *The Strange Bird* by Adèle Geras first published by Hamish Hamilton Ltd 1988, copyright © Adèle Geras, 1988, reprinted by kind permission of the author c/o Laura Cecil Agency; 'The Way Out' by Joyce Dunbar from *Bedtime Stories for the Very Young* first published by Kingfisher Books 1991, copyright © Joyce Dunbar, 1991, reprinted by kind permission of the author c/o David Higham Associates Ltd; 'The Wonderful Smell' by Shoo Rayner from *Cyril's Cat and the Big Surprise* first published in Puffin Books 1993, copyright © Shoo Rayner, 1993, reprinted by permission of Penguin Books Ltd; 'The Elephant's Picnic' by Richard Hughes from *Animal Stories* first published by Orchard 1992, copyright © Richard Hughes, 1992, reprinted by kind permission of the author c/o David Higham Associates Ltd; 'A Fish of the World' by Terry Jones from *Fairy Tales* first published by Pavilion Books Ltd 1981, copyright © Terry Jones, 1981, reprinted by permission of Pavilion Books Ltd; 'Tortoise Longs to Fly' by Hiawyn Oram from *Counting Leopard's Spots* first published by Orchard Books, 1996, copyright © Hiawyn Oram, 1996, reprinted by permission of Orchard Books, a division of the Watts Publishing Group, 96 Leonard Street, London, EC2A 4RH; 'The Mouse's Bridegroom' by Barbara Ker Wilson from *The Puffin Bedtime Story Book* first published by Penguin Books Australia Ltd 1990, copyright © Barbara Ker Wilson, 1987, reprinted by permission of the Macquarie Library Pty Ltd.

Every effort has been made to trace the copyright holders. The publisher would like to hear from any copyright holder not acknowledged.